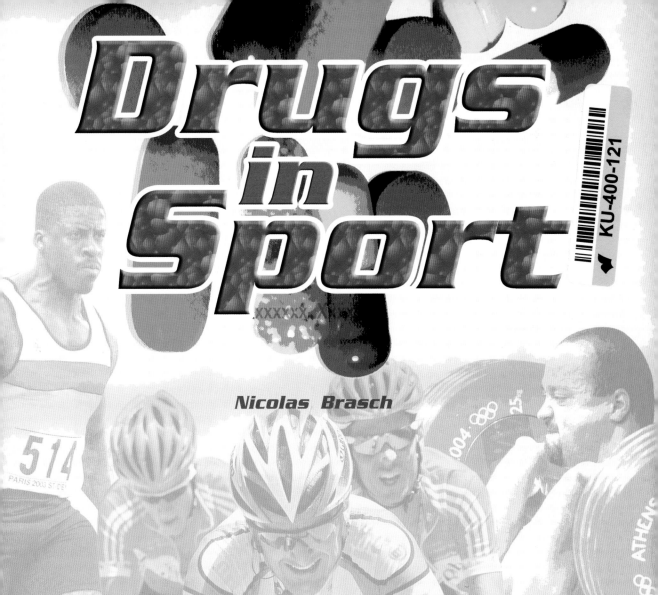

Drugs in Sport

Nicolas Brasch

Nelson Thornes

Nelson Thornes

First published in 2007 by Cengage Learning Australia
www.cengage.com.au

This edition published in 2008 under the imprint of Nelson Thornes Ltd,
Delta Place, 27 Bath Road, Cheltenham, United Kingdom, GL53 7TH

10 9 8 7 6 5 4 3 2
11 10 09 08

Drugs in Sport
ISBN 978-1-4085-0130-6

Text by Nicolas Brasch
Edited by Bec Quinn
Designed by James Lowe
Series Design by James Lowe
Production Controller Seona Galbally
Photo Research by Fiona Smith
Audio recordings by Juliet Hill, Picture Start
Spoken by Matthew King and Abbe Holmes
Printed in China by 1010 Printing International Ltd

Website www.nelsonthornes.com

Acknowledgements
The author and publisher would like to acknowledge permission to reproduce material from
the following sources:
Photographs by AAP Image/AFP/Niurka Barroso, pp. 17 top, back cover bottom; AAP Image/AP Photo/
Greg Baker, p. 15; AAP Image/AP Photo/Tony Feder, p. 18; Corbis/Leo Mason, p. 14; Corbis/Tim De
Waele, p. 16; Getty Images/AFP, p. 7; Getty Images/AFP/Alessandro Abbonizio, p. 21; Getty Images/AFP/
Franck Fife, pp. front cover centre, 10, 22; Getty Images/AFP/Javier Soriano, pp. 4, 8; Getty Images/AFP/
Jeff Haynes, p. 5; Getty Images/AFP/Ramzi Haidar, pp. front cover right, 11, 23 right; Getty Images/AFP/
Rob Elliott, pp. 14-15; Getty Images/AFP/Romeo Gacad, pp. 3, 9; Getty Images/Allsport/Simon Bruty,
pp. 10-11, 23 centre bottom; Getty Images/Graeme Robertson, p. 20; Getty Images/Phil Cole, pp. front
cover left, 19, 23 left; Getty Images/Thomas E. Witte, p. 6; iStockphoto.com, p. 13; Photolibrary/Alamy/
Doug Steley, pp. 17 centre; back cover top; Photolibrary/Science Photo Library/Adam Hart-Davis,
pp. 12-13; Photolibrary/Science Photo Library/Dr. P. Marazzi, p. 12.

Drugs in Sport

Nicolas Brasch

Contents

Chapter 1

PERFORMANCE-ENHANCING DRUGS

Some sportspeople try to improve their chances of winning by using drugs.

The drugs sportspeople use aren't drugs that drug takers in the community take, and they aren't drugs that change people's thoughts.

They're drugs that **enhance** a person's performance.

Drugs that enhance performance
make a person's body go faster,
or become stronger than it normally would be.
These drugs are known as performance-enhancing drugs.
There are many different performance-enhancing drugs.
These drugs have no place in sport today.

Chapter 2

WHY SPORTSPEOPLE USE DRUGS

Sportspeople who use performance-enhancing drugs take them to improve their performance.

They want to improve their performance because of the **glory** and rewards that come from being a sporting success.

Serena Williams' natural talent has made her a sporting success.

People who reach the top of a sport can become famous and earn a lot of money.

David Beckham has reached the top of his sport without using performance-enhancing drugs.

Some sportspeople who use performance-enhancing drugs take them because they don't have the natural talent to reach the top. They need extra help to win.

In cycling and athletics, the real champions don't use performance-enhancing drugs.

Some sportspeople take performance-enhancing drugs
to compete against other drug takers.
They believe they also have to take the drugs to win.

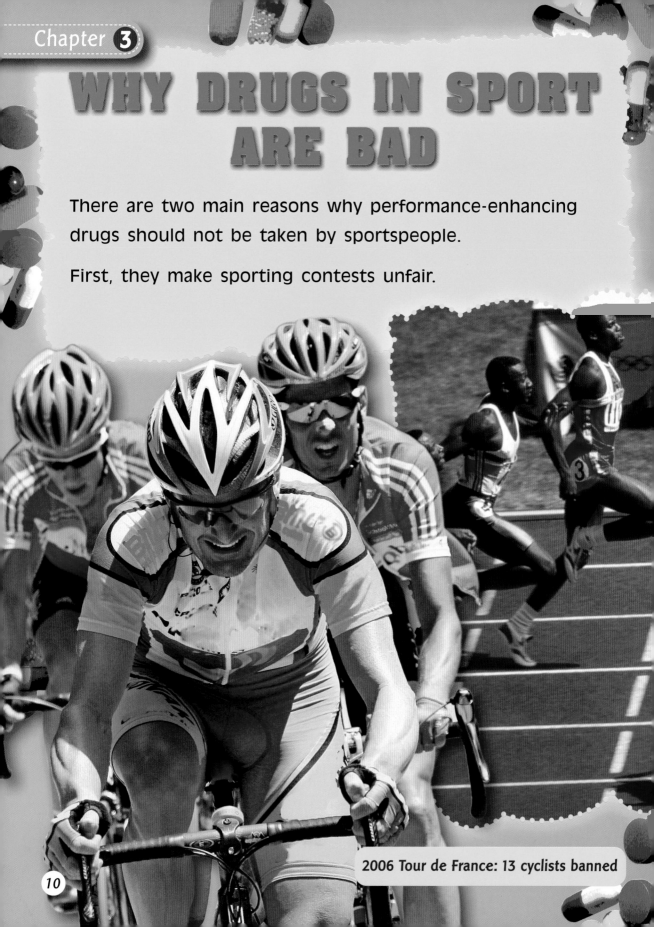

Chapter 3

WHY DRUGS IN SPORT ARE BAD

There are two main reasons why performance-enhancing drugs should not be taken by sportspeople.

First, they make sporting contests unfair.

2006 Tour de France: 13 cyclists banned

They give the drug takers an unfair **advantage**.

Sportspeople who take drugs can run faster,
or lift heavier weights, or compete for longer.
That's unfair.

It's not what sport is about.

Seoul Olympics: Ben Johnson banned

Athens Olympics: Ferenc Gyurkovics banned

Second, performance-enhancing drugs **cause** side-effects. Some cause only a bit of pain to the people taking them, but many cause damage to a person's body.

Side-effects include:

- stomach pain
- nausea
- acne

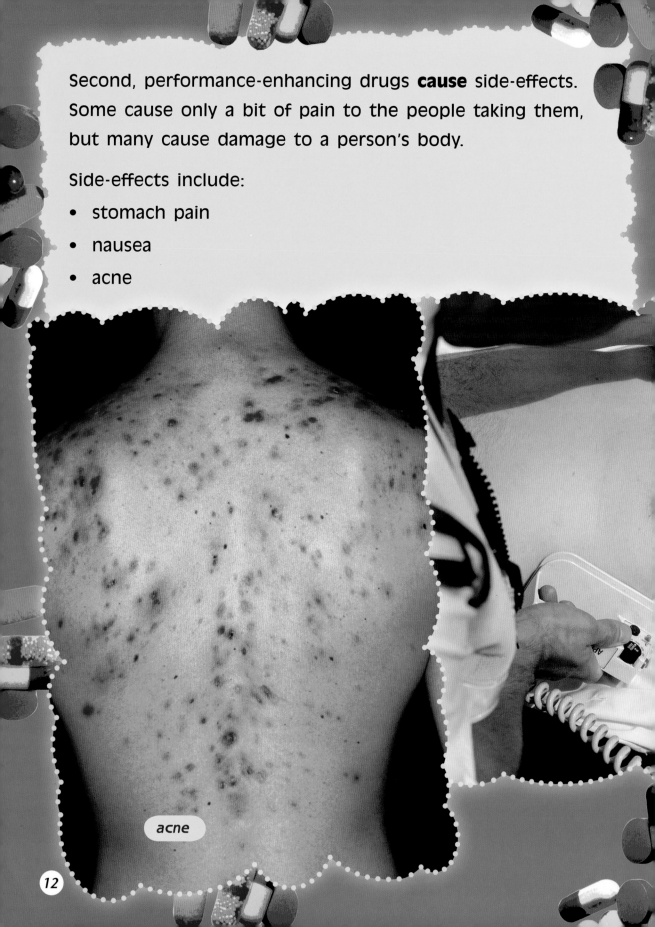

acne

- fertility problems
- deep voice (for females)
- stunted growth (for teenagers)
- stroke
- seizure
- heart attack.

In some cases, sportspeople have died from these side-effects.

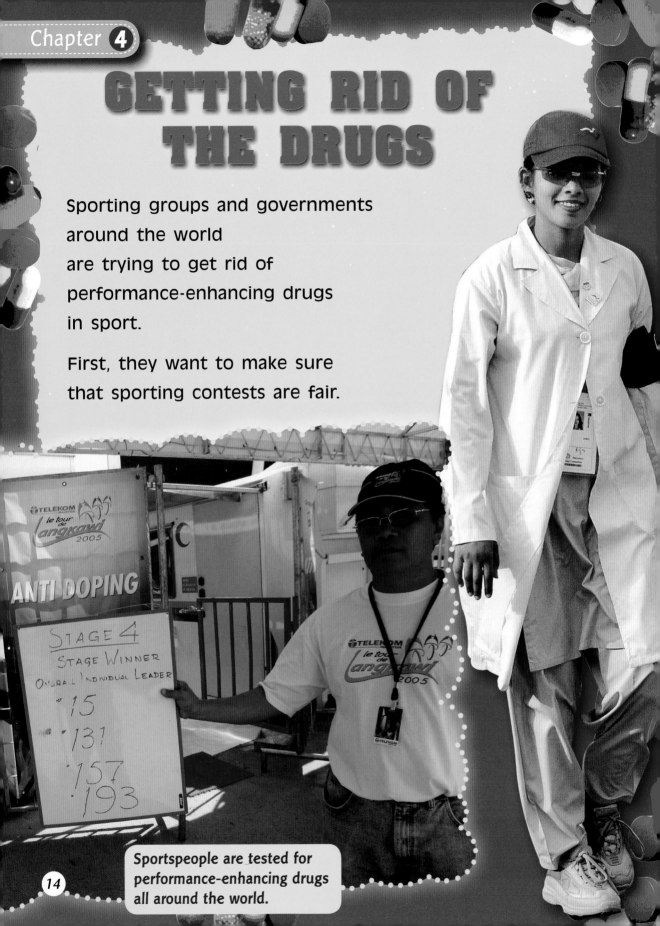

Chapter **4**

GETTING RID OF THE DRUGS

Sporting groups and governments around the world are trying to get rid of performance-enhancing drugs in sport.

First, they want to make sure that sporting contests are fair.

Sportspeople are tested for performance-enhancing drugs all around the world.

ANTI DOPING

STAGE 4
STAGE WINNER
OVERALL INDIVIDUAL LEADER
15
131
157
193

Second, they don't want sportspeople to have serious medical problems or to die from taking performance-enhancing drugs.

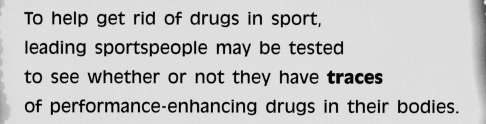

To help get rid of drugs in sport, leading sportspeople may be tested to see whether or not they have **traces** of performance-enhancing drugs in their bodies.

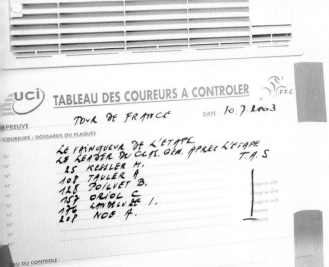

a cyclist waits for a drug test during the Tour de France

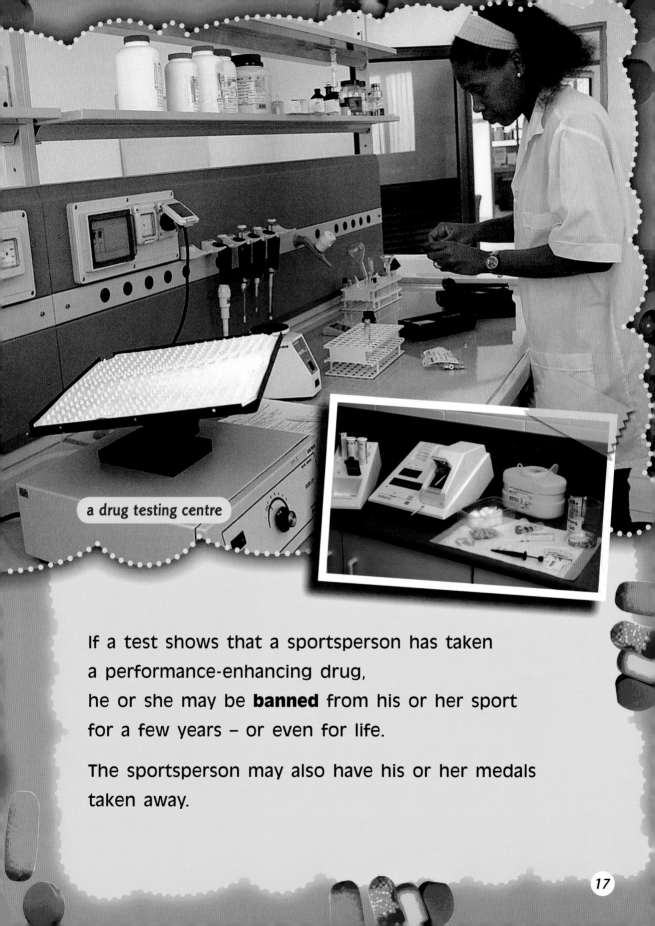

a drug testing centre

If a test shows that a sportsperson has taken
a performance-enhancing drug,
he or she may be **banned** from his or her sport
for a few years – or even for life.

The sportsperson may also have his or her medals
taken away.

Chapter 5

DWAIN CHAMBERS

Dwain Chambers is a British sprinter who took performance-enhancing drugs.

Dwain won several medals in the 100-metre sprint and sprint relay.

Dwain was banned from his sport for two years because he was caught
taking performance-enhancing drugs.

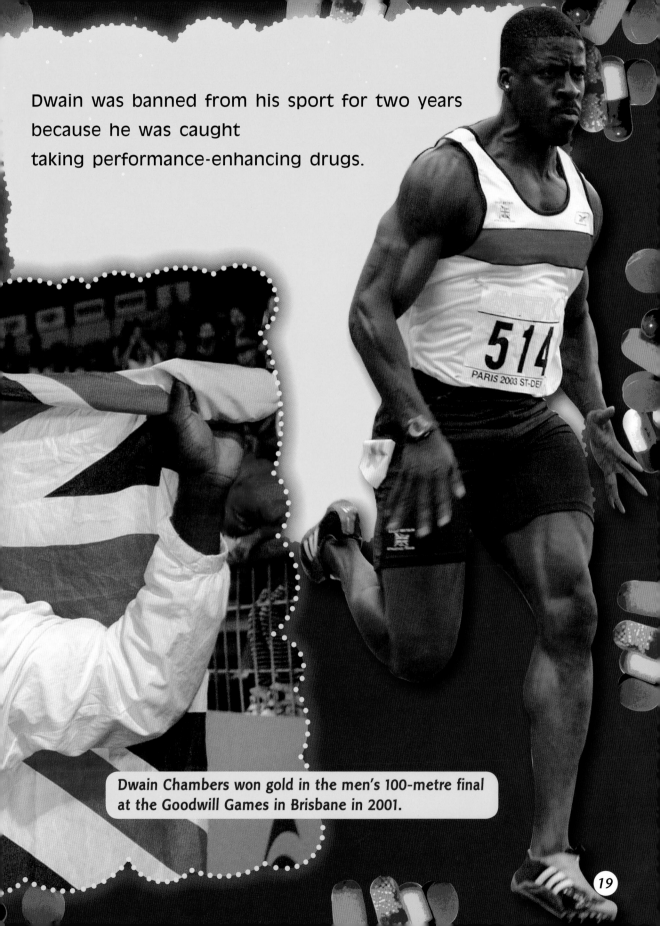

Dwain Chambers won gold in the men's 100-metre final at the Goodwill Games in Brisbane in 2001.

In an interview Dwain Chambers gave in 2005,
he said:

"Everything I had worked for since I was 14 years old
had totally **vanished**...
It's not the way I want people to see me –
I've got a black mark against my name now
as a drugs cheat..."

Dwain Chambers waiting
for the result of his trial

"There's nobody else I can blame,
for the simple reason that I made those decisions
to go forward as I did…
I was young, I didn't think about life
and the ups and downs that could occur."

Chapter 6

CONCLUSION

Performance-enhancing drugs are banned in sport because they give the sportspeople who take them an unfair advantage over other sportspeople.

They can also cause a lot of harm to people who take them.
They can even cause people to die.

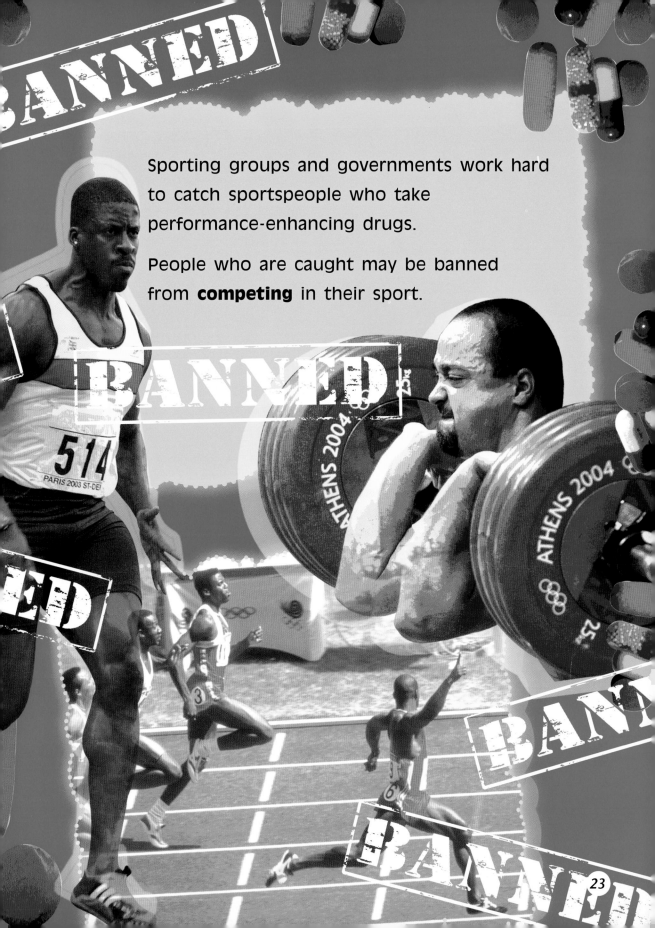

Sporting groups and governments work hard to catch sportspeople who take performance-enhancing drugs.

People who are caught may be banned from **competing** in their sport.

Glossary

advantage a lead; benefit

banned stopped from competing

cause bring about

competing taking part in a contest

enhance improve

glory praise

traces small amounts

vanished disappeared; gone away

Index